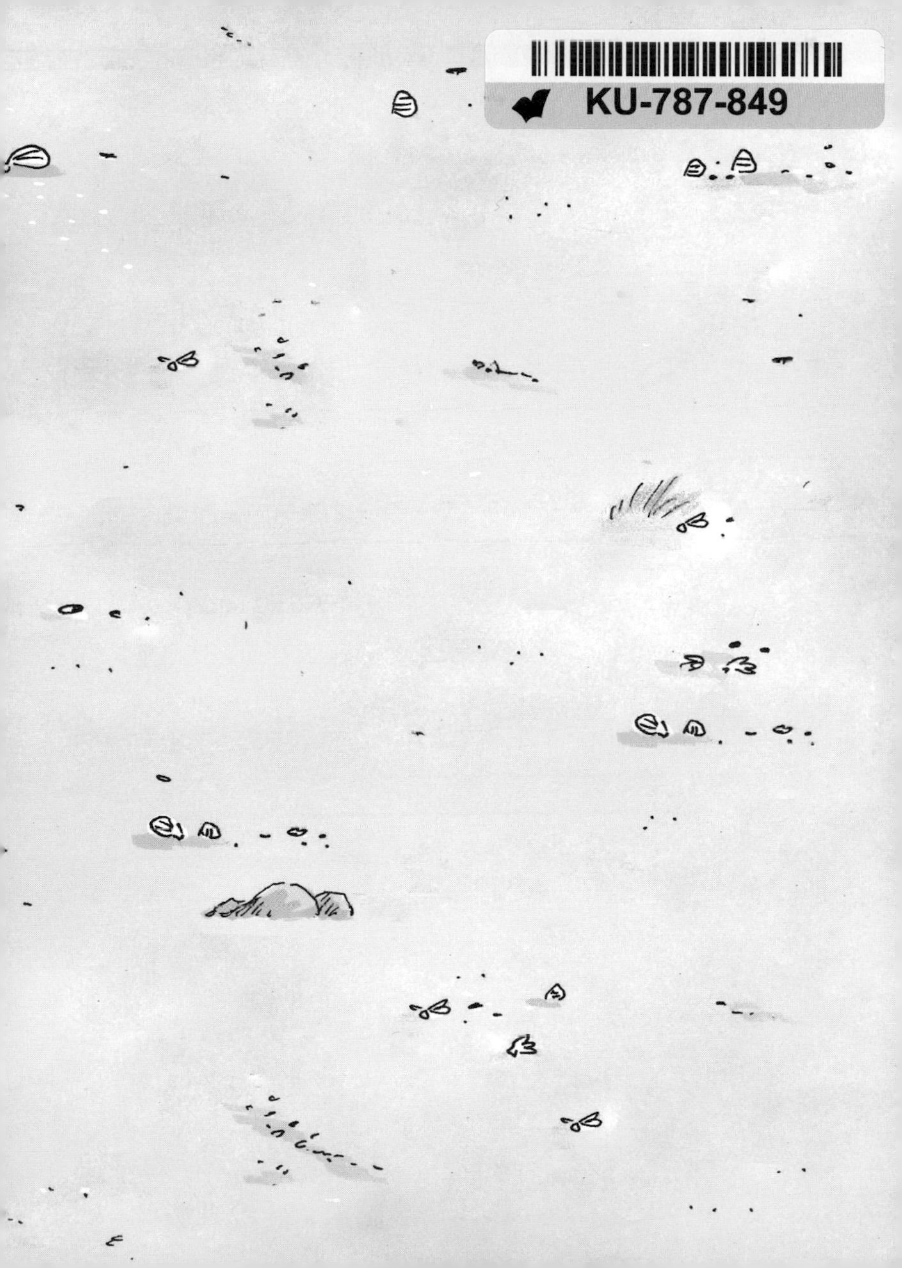

The Beach Puppy

The Beach Puppy

HOLLY WEBB

Illustrated by
Ellie Snowdon

Barrington Stoke

First published in 2021 in Great Britain by
Barrington Stoke Ltd
18 Walker Street, Edinburgh, EH3 7LP

www.barringtonstoke.co.uk

Text © 2021 Holly Webb
Illustrations © 2021 Ellie Snowdon

A CIP catalogue record for this book is available
from the British Library upon request

ISBN: 978-1-78112-950-0

Printed by Hussar Books, Poland

This book is in a super-readable format for young readers
beginning their independent reading journey.

For Martha

Contents

Chapter 1

A Special Surprise

Coco felt the dog crate shake again as she was lifted out of the car. She made a sad noise and scratched at the front of the crate. She wanted to be back with her mum and the other puppies at the shelter.

The door of the dog crate creaked open. Coco didn't know what was going on, and she pressed herself back into the dark box.

"Come on out, little one," a man's voice called softly to Coco.

"What is it, Dad?" said another voice from outside the crate.

"It's a surprise. A special surprise for you, Ruby ..." the man's voice said.

Coco saw a girl crouch down next to the door of her crate.

"A puppy, Dad! For me?"

Coco padded to the door. The girl sounded so happy, and Coco wanted to see what was happening.

"Oh, she's so sweet!" Ruby said. "A sausage dog! Mum, look at her! She's so little."

Ruby's mum bent down next to the crate. "We know you love sausage dogs, Ruby," Mum said. "And you've been so good since I had Sam. It's not always easy having a baby brother. We wanted you to have someone special to play with and look after."

"She's coming out … Is she coming to see us?" Ruby asked.

Coco could see that Ruby's eyes were wide and excited.

"What's her name?" asked Ruby.

"At the shelter they called her Coco," Dad said. "I think it's a great name for her."

"It's perfect. Hey, Coco ..." Ruby put out her hand and Coco slowly sniffed her fingers. Then she nudged Ruby's hand with her nose and wagged her tail. She put her front paws up on Ruby's knee and looked around. Coco wasn't sure what was happening, but she did know that these people were kind.

Chapter 2

Off to the Beach

Coco soon forgot her time at the shelter. She felt as though she had lived with Ruby and her family always. She loved going for walks with Ruby and cuddling up with her to watch TV or read a book. But now something odd was happening. The whole house was full of bags and

piles of stuff, and everyone seemed to be excited ...

"Oh!" Ruby tugged at her bag's zip again, but it was no good – the bag was not going to close. She gave a sigh. "I'm just going to have to take some things out," she told Coco.

The little sausage dog peered into the bag and thumped her tail on Ruby's duvet.

"It's so hard to know what to pack," Ruby said, pulling out some books and a squishy, limp blow-up dinosaur swim toy. "A week's a long time, and you need loads of stuff at the beach."

Coco put her paws up on the side of the bag and sniffed. Then the sausage dog reached in and found her favourite yellow ball. It was tucked inside one of Ruby's trainers.

Ruby squeaked. "I know! I'll tell Mum you need your own bag. It's not fair I have to take all your stuff too. Sam's got his own bag, and his nappy bag, and a cot, and a bag of toys, and he's not that much bigger than you."

*

In the back of the car, Coco wriggled round inside her crate and dug her paws into the blanket that Ruby had put in there for her to lie on. She felt as if she'd been shut in the crate for hours and was getting very fed up. And she was hungry.

She whined loudly, and Ruby leaned over to look. "Ssshhh … It's OK, Coco. Not much longer." Ruby turned round to talk to her dad. "Are we nearly there, Dad?" she asked.

"We're so nearly there, I promise," Ruby's dad called from the front of the car.

"Look, you can see the sea," Mum said, and Ruby bounced in her seat and whooped. Coco didn't know what was happening, but she barked to join in.

"This is it – our cottage!" Dad said as he parked the car outside a small pink-painted house right at the top of the cliff.

Coco jumped and squirmed as Ruby opened up the crate and clipped on her lead. "We're here!" Ruby told her. "Look, Coco – that's the beach down there! And the sea!"

Chapter 3

Splashing and Jumping

Down on the beach later that morning, Ruby jumped back from the edge of the sea. "Oh! It's cold!" she laughed as the waves washed towards them.

The water swirled around Coco's paws. It was her first time at the seaside, and she was feeling a bit nervous. Coco tugged hard on her lead and tried to pull Ruby back up the beach away from the waves.

"Don't you like it?" Ruby asked as she bent down beside her. "It's fun, Coco. Don't be scared."

Coco looked at the sea and sniffed. She didn't know what to think about all that water. She took a very small step forwards and barked at the waves.

She liked the beach very much – the sand was excellent for digging, and she had made some big holes already. She loved the smelly seaweed and crab shells and seagull feathers all along

the tideline. It was just the sea that worried her.

Coco watched as Ruby's dad came down to the water and began to wade in.

Ruby watched too, dancing about on the sand, and then handed Coco's lead to her mum. "Dad, wait for me! I'm coming in too!"

She splashed into the water,
squeaking at the cold, and Coco saw
the sea swallow her up – feet and legs,
all the way to her tummy! Coco whined
and pulled hard at the lead. What was
happening to Ruby? She didn't like
this at all.

Ruby was splashing and jumping,
and Coco was sure that the water was
hurting her. She growled.

"It's OK, Coco," Mum told her, but Coco wasn't having it. She pulled again, even harder, and Mum lost her balance. She let go of the lead, and Coco dashed into the sea.

She wasn't going to let the water take Ruby!

Chapter 4

So Much to See

Ruby watched as Coco splashed and scrabbled – and swam towards her!

"Coco! You can swim! Dad, look, isn't she clever?" Ruby made her way back towards the little sausage dog, but then Coco tried to get out of the water using Ruby as her ladder.

"Ow, ow, your claws hurt!" Ruby squeaked.

As soon as Coco had made sure that Ruby was OK, she calmed down. She wriggled away and swam about, paddling between Ruby and Dad.

It was too cold to stay in the sea for very long, so Ruby thought she'd make a massive sandcastle instead.

Coco helped. She dug out the moat, and Ruby decorated the castle with sparkly white pebbles. The castle was almost finished when a boy ran past too close. He bumped the castle with his foot, and the whole side fell in.

Ruby looked horrified, and Coco barked at him, but he didn't even stop to say sorry.

"Never mind, Ruby, you can build it again after lunch," her mum called. "Come and have a sandwich."

Ruby tried to see where the boy had gone, but he'd already vanished.

*

After lunch, Ruby's dad said they
should go along the beach to look at the
lighthouse. As they tramped over the
sand, Coco sniffed at all the picnics and
a delicious-looking dead fish, which Ruby
wouldn't let her eat.

Then Coco spotted a kite dancing in
the air up ahead. She stared at it and
then darted forward. The kite bounced
and twirled. Coco wanted so much to
chase it. She raced after it, but the kite
spun up high above her, too high for
Coco to reach.

Coco didn't mind. There was so much else to look at. She pushed her nose deep into a pile of smelly seaweed and then went to bark at the waves. They kept running away, which was good.

Then Coco looked round to make sure that Ruby hadn't gone into the sea again without Coco to protect her.

But Ruby wasn't there. No one was there. No one was holding the end of her lead.

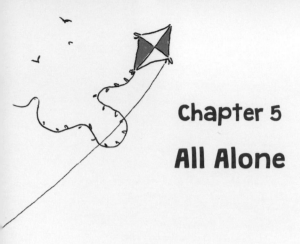

Chapter 5

All Alone

Coco stood by the sea, all on her own. She wagged her tail, but she was puzzled. Where was Ruby? Where was Dad? She didn't understand.

She looked back down the beach, but she couldn't see Ruby or Dad anywhere.

The sea rushed in and wet her paws, and Coco darted back with a yelp.

She had to find Ruby. She needed Ruby.

She would just have to hunt for them. They must be nearby.

Coco trotted back along the beach, listening out for Ruby calling her. But there were so many people shouting and laughing, she couldn't pick out Ruby's voice at all.

Coco began to worry – was she even going the right way?

Which way was their picnic rug, and Mum and Sam? Coco stood looking up and down the beach and sniffed the air. First there had been the kite, and then she'd stopped to sniff the seaweed ... It was ... that way. Wasn't it?

"Hey! Where's your owner?" shouted a boy. Coco jumped back as he reached down to grab her lead. She knew him! It was the boy who'd kicked the sandcastle and made Ruby sad.

"Come back here!" the boy yelled, and this time he stamped one foot firmly down on Coco's lead.

Coco hardly ever growled, but she growled now and snapped her teeth. She didn't want that boy anywhere near her.

She wriggled and pulled – and yanked her head right through her collar. Then she shot away along the beach, leaving the horrible boy holding her collar and lead.

Chapter 6

Where's Coco?

Further back along the beach, Ruby was picking herself up from the sand and brushing it off her shorts. "Are you all right, Ruby?" Dad asked as he helped her up. "You haven't hurt yourself?"

Ruby shook her head, laughing. "I'm OK – I was looking at the kite, and I just didn't see that big hole in the sand."

"Someone should fill it in," Dad said, looking cross. "It's not safe."

"Hey!" Ruby looked around. "Dad, where's Coco? I dropped her lead!"

Dad blinked and then turned round to look too. "Oh, wow, I forgot all about her! I was worrying about you. Coco! Coco, here, girl! She can't be far ..."

But Coco was nowhere to be seen.

"We have to find her," Ruby said as she ran along the beach. "Have you seen my dog?" she asked a man building a sandcastle with a little girl. "A sausage dog? She ran off ..."

"I saw her!" the little girl said. "She went that way! She's cute!"

"Thanks," Ruby gasped, and dashed on.

Plenty of people had seen a little dog running past, but always just a few minutes before Ruby and Dad got there. No one knew where Coco had gone.

Then, when they were halfway along the beach and Ruby was almost crying with worry, she heard Dad catch his breath. "What is it?" Ruby asked.

Dad reached down and held up a bright red collar and lead.

*

As Dad and Ruby searched for her, Coco was sitting behind a pile of buckets and spades outside the beach cafe. She was panting, and her heart was still thumping. She couldn't see the horrible boy anywhere, but if she went back out on to the sand, he might chase her again.

She wanted so much to dash out and keep on hunting for Ruby. But every time she tried to move from behind the buckets she was sure she could hear the boy's voice shouting down on the beach, so she hid again.

She had to go, she had to find Ruby ...

Coco edged her nose out round the bright plastic buckets and looked up and down the beach one more time. She couldn't see or hear the boy.

Maybe it was safe ...

Chapter 7

Time to Go

"We can't go home yet!" Ruby cried
a couple of hours later. She couldn't
believe that Mum and Dad were packing
up to go back to the cottage. "Please!
We have to find Coco first. We can't just
leave her!"

"I promise we'll come back," Dad said.

"I'm sorry, Ruby." Mum came over to hug her. "I don't want to leave Coco either. But we've been looking for a long time, and Sam's really tired and hungry. We need to get him his tea and put him to bed. Once you and Dad have helped me carry everything up the steps to the cottage, you can come back and keep looking, I promise."

Ruby gave a sigh. Mum was right – Sam was grizzling and rubbing his eyes. It wouldn't be long before he started to howl.

"I'm coming," she muttered, and picked up the bag of beach towels and her bucket and spade.

She went with Mum and Dad across the sand to the steps and then turned to look back.

The beach was almost empty now.
Families were trailing home with all
their bags. Some of them had a last ice
cream in their hands too. Ruby stood
and watched them, hoping to spot Coco.
How could she leave without her dog?

They had been so happy and excited that morning when they carried all the bags down these same steps. Everything was different now. Even the pretty beach huts looked sad and grubby.

Ruby looked down the beach one last time. Maybe she'd see a little black and tan sausage dog racing over the sand towards her, barking with happiness. But there were no dogs at all, just seagulls wheeling and screeching.

Ruby gulped down tears and began to climb the steps.

Chapter 8

Just in Time

Even though Ruby wasn't able to see Coco, the little dog was still there, hiding in front of the beach cafe.

Coco looked up and down the sand again and again. And then suddenly she thought she saw Ruby, far away along the beach.

Coco's tail began to thump against the sandy ground, and as she leaned forward, her nose began to twitch. It *was* Ruby! Coco was sure of it!

She shot out of her hiding place in front of the cafe, and the buckets fell around her with a crash.

She raced along the path in front of the beach huts, faster than she'd ever run before.

Every little bit of her was fixed on Ruby, that tiny person in the distance. She wasn't really looking at anything in between.

Coco ran right through a family who were getting one last ice cream on their way home from the beach. She hardly saw them.

"Hey! What was that?"

"What's that dog doing?"

"Alfie, watch out!"

The littlest boy tripped over Coco and dropped his ice cream with a howl.

Coco darted away in panic. She didn't understand what she'd done, and everyone was shouting at her. She hid underneath one of the beach huts and shivered.

When she came out, it was too late.

Ruby was gone.

*

Ruby was following Mum and Dad up the steps to the top of the cliff, but she kept looking back down at the beach, looking for Coco.

"Oh no!" Mum turned and tried to grab Sam's stripy blanket. It was his favourite one, the one he snuggled with to sleep. Now it was blowing away down the steps.

"Ruby, can you catch it?" Dad called.

Ruby reached out as it flew past her, but her arm just wasn't long enough. She dumped the bag and ran back down the steps after the blanket. They couldn't lose that too.

She pounded along the path and grabbed the blanket as it was about to end up under a beach hut. Everything was dirty and dusty under there; she'd caught it just in time. Ruby crouched there panting for a moment, and then her eyes widened.

Staring back at her was a tiny,
whiskery black and tan face.

"Coco!" she breathed.

Coco scrambled out of her hiding place, whining and squeaking. Her tail made little sandy clouds on the path as she covered Ruby's face with licky kisses.

"Where did you go?" Ruby whispered, picking her up and snuggling her tight. "We looked and looked. Oh, Coco, I'm so glad to see you."

Coco put her nose deep into Ruby's hair and sighed with love.

PILLGWENLLY